What Do Giraffes Eat?

Written by **Greg Wachs**
Illustrated by **Rituparna & Pratyush Chatterjee**
Published by **Funky Dreamer Storytime**

D1302742

What Do Giraffes Eat?

Printed in the United States of America.
First Printing, 2018

ISBN-13: 978-1983463662   ISBN-10: 1983463663
Published by **Funky Dreamer Storytime**
Funky Dreamer Storytime
Greg Wachs
139 North Laurel Ave.
Los Angeles, CA 90048
www.funkydreamerstorytime.com
310-966-7536
greg@funkydreamerstorytime.com
mediacom2020@gmail.com
Twitter: @podcasts4kids

Rituparna & Pratyush Chatterjee can be reached
via Upwork.com or at ritu_vns8119@yahoo.com and
pratyushji79@gmail.com

Amir Mortel can be reached via Upwork.com or at
amircmortel@gmail.com

Ordering Information

Special discounts are available on quantity purchases
by corporations, education, K12, and associations. For
details, contact the publisher at the info above. Orders
by bookstores and wholesalers, please contact us at
the info above.

Matching Podcast available on **iTunes** and at
www.funkydreamerstorytime.com

Dedication

*This book is dedicated to the teachers of the world,
who work hard everyday to enrich our children's lives.
Thank you for all that you do!*

– Greg Wachs

*I dedicate this book to my husband, Pratyush, for always
making me the best that I can be!*

– Rituparna Chatterjee

What do monkeys eat?

Bananas!

Can you count the bananas?

What do eagles eat?

Fish!

Can you count the fish?

What do giraffes eat?

Leaves!

Can you count the leaves?

What do mice eat?

Cheese!

Can you count the pieces of cheese?

What do rabbits eat?

Carrots!

Can you count the carrots?

What do kids eat?

Ice cream!

Can you count the ice cream cones?

Um... Didn't you mean to say that kids eat BROCCOLI???

Can you count the pieces of broccoli?

Yes we eat broccoli,
but we also eat
ICE CREAM!!!

Can you count the ice cream cones, AGAIN?

What do they eat?

About the Author

Greg Wachs is a children's book author, podcast creator and musician living in West Hollywood, CA with his wife, Shula and daughter, Ananbelle Rae.

About the Illustrators

For over ten years, Rituparna and Pratyush Chatterjee have formed a niche as illustrators and cartoonists in the world of arts and entertainment. They both have Commercial Art degrees and are well known for their expertise in Print Publication and Digital Media. Rituparna and Pratyush live in India, with their 3 year old daughter.

Remember Kids these are, "Pod-Books",
which means they have a matching podcast!

Just go to www.funkydreamerstorytime.com
or search **iTunes** for the name of the book.

Each podcast reads you the book.
They are also chock full of really cool music!

**So, fire up a podcast, kick back
and enjoy the adventure!**